GECKO PRESS

DON'T CROSS THE LINE!

THIS IS HOW IT'S GOING TO BE. GIVE THE ORDERS AROUND HERE!

ISABEL MINHÓ MARTINS · BERNARDO P. CARVALHO

TRANSLATED BY DANIEL HAHN

TOMMY

SiMON   CRiSTiANO

STEVE

BERNARDO

YARA

iGOR

HONEY

MARiA

RUSSO

LUCAS

BOO

OFFiCER AMARAL

CHiCO

CARLA

BOB   JORGE

iSiDORO   SALGADO

LOUiS BUNNY

MR. ALBiNO

NUNO

JOHN

NELO

DAViD

MR. SANTOS SOUSA

IZZY

RUi   CLARA   JOE ?

THIS EDITION FIRST PUBLISHED IN 2016 BY
GECKO PRESS
PO BOX 9335 MARION SQUARE
WELLINGTON 6141, NEW ZEALAND
INFO@GECKOPRESS.COM

TEXT © ISABEL MINHÓS MARTINS
ILLUSTRATIONS © BERNARDO P. CARVALHO
ENGLISH LANGUAGE EDITION © GECKOPRESS LTD 2016
TRANSLATION © DANIEL HAHN
THIS EDITION IS PUBLISHED UNDER
LICENCE FROM EDITORA
PLANETA TANGERINA
PORTUGAL

DISTRIBUTED IN THE UNITED STATES AND CANADA
BY LERNER PUBLISHING GROUP
WWW.LERNERBOOKS.COM
DISTRIBUTED IN THE UNITED KINGDOM
BY BOUNCE SALES AND MARKETING
WWW.BOUNCEMARKETING.CO.UK
DISTRIBUTED IN AUSTRALIA
BY SCHOLASTIC AUSTRALIA,
WWW.SCHOLASTIC.COM.AU
DISTRIBUTED IN NEW ZEALAND
BY UPSTART DISTRIBUTION
WWW.UPSTARTPRESS.CO.NZ
EDITED BY PENELOPE TODD
TYPE SETTING BY VIDA & LUKE KELLY, NEW ZEALAND
PRINTED IN CHINA BY
EVERBEST PRINTING CO.LTD
AN ACCREDITED ISO 14001 & FSC
CERTIFIED PRINTER
WWW.GECKOPRESS.COM

FUNDING ASSISTANCE FROM THE
DIREÇÃO-GERAL DO LIVRO
DOS ARQUIVOS E DAS BIBLITECAS

DG
LB
DIRECÇÃO-GERAL
DO LIVRO E DAS
BIBLIOTECAS

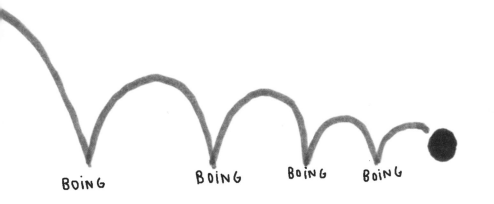

BOING   BOING   BOING   BOING

ME?

MARCO   SILVA   COSTA   RAFAEL   MADALENA   THE GUARD   GRUNF   LAETITIA

VIVI   ANA K.   HENRY   CAROL   MARCELINO   MR. SANTINO   ISABEL   BABO

JACK   VICTOR   NEIGHING-ROCKET   5   4   3   2   1   MOTHER

GENERAL
ALCAZAR   MIRO   EDMUND   CHRIS   SAMUEL   PAT   PAULINA